The Peephole

Check out the other books in the

FRIGHTVISION

series:

FRIGHTVISION

The Peephole

Culliver Crantz

J
FRIGHTVISION

Cover illustration: Stephanie Gaston
Cover Design: Stephanie Gaston

www.FrightVisionBooks.com

Instagram & Facebook: @FrightVisionBooks

Dearest Visitor,

Welcome!

Everyone loses something at some point in their lives ... It could be as simple as a toy or something more.

Would you be willing to give up everything to get back what you lost?

Or will you face the unknown?

Your nightmare is ready. Let's begin!

Sweetest Dreams,

Crantz

CHAPTER ONE

"No! No! No!" I slammed my fist into my bed as tears mixed with snot and rage fell down my face. I couldn't stop. It seemed like I had been punching my bed for days, wishing that things would be different.

Four days ago, I lost my best friend. And not in the woods. He died. He was gone forever and yesterday was his funeral. That was the hardest day of my life.

One week ago we were at camp together, decked out in our Space Camp t-shirts, having the time of our lives, and planning out every space adventure that we were going to have in the future ... like we did every summer. I can picture Tom in that shirt—he never took it off. Space Camp always led to our joint birthday party. Next month I turn twelve years old—

Tom was supposed to also. We had the same birthday—the Fourth of July.

Instead of planning another awesome party, I was left devastated, crushed, and angry. Deep down, I knew that Tom wouldn't want me to feel like that because of his death, but I couldn't stop myself. The only thing that kept me going was the promise that I made to him five days ago—the last time I saw him.

"What happened?" I had asked Tom, in shock, while processing seeing my best friend wrapped in bandages and hooked up to hospital machines. I could barely see his Space Camp shirt—the same one that we both wore just days before.

"I was trying to bring your space shuttle over to your house. You left it in my bag from Space Camp," Tom groaned. "I was on my bike ... headed to your house. Then I ended up here."

"What hit you?" I had asked Tom, while standing at the foot of his hospital bed.

"Someone saw a pickup truck. It, it blew through a stop sign, then crashed into ... the side of my bike. I can kinda remember seeing something ... red. Something red coming towards me. It's fuzzy. Then I woke up in the hospital." Tom could barely move as the heart monitor that he was hooked up to reacted to his movements.

"What? Someone did this and then took off?"

Tom had nodded.

I was enraged. My head spun. "Does anyone know who?"

"No. Not yet."

My blood had boiled with anger. "No … no … this is not okay. I'm gonna find out who did this, I promise."

That was it. The last time I saw him.

I shot up in bed. I had to figure out who was responsible for this—who was driving the red truck?

I quickly put clothes on, rushed out of my room, and down the stairs. I yelled "Bye!" to Mom and before long I was on my bike, pedaling through town. I needed to know who caused Tom's death. How could they do it and why?

I rode around the area and eventually past Tom's house, retracing the path that he would have taken to get to my house on his bike. No red trucks in any driveway. There was an orange cone though, about two blocks over from where my house was. Next to that were some flowers. That was where the accident had happened. Where Tom got hit on his bike as he rode to my house to give me my model space shuttle toy from our last time at Space Camp.

I stopped riding and pulled to the side of the road. My bike crashed to the ground as I got off it and touched the street. Like a bloodhound on a scent, I crouched low, looking back and forth. Back and forth.

Poor Tom, I thought. *How could this happen to him and here, so close to both of our houses?*

I hopped back on my bike and pedaled as fast as I could. I flew past Tom's house again, to the next neighborhood, and the one after that. It was all I could do. I just kept going.

The sun was setting. Usually, I went home before dark, but there was no chance of that today. I was still going in the opposite direction of my house, riding at warp speed, as if I were on a spaceship to visit Tom.

I reached a steep hill and biked up it with ease. Dark, ominous clouds rushed in as I neared the top. I wasn't scared. Wind whipped around me, trying to make things difficult, as if something supernatural was trying to stop me from going farther—it seemed like something knew where I was headed.

My visibility got worse and worse as lights and houses became sparse. Darkness took over the once bright sky, but I made it. I got off my bike as I had reached a trail in the woods.

This was the spot I had been looking for—a place that was very important to Tom and me. I stared up at the steep hill through the woods. In my head, I could hear Tom calling out: "3, 2, 1 … blast off!"

Hearing that made me think of every time that we came here. We'd both stand at the bottom of the hill and count down from three, then we'd charge up the hill.

I wasn't sure if I really heard it just now or if my mind was trained to hear that whenever I came here.

Was it really him or was my mind playing tricks on me?

I had to find out.

I began my climb through the hilly woods.

Crickets chirped.

An owl hooted.

Cicadas buzzed.

None of that was going to stop me. I was headed to an abandoned cabin deep in the woods—our cabin, the one where Tom and I talked about all of our space dreams. If he was going to be anywhere, he was going to be there.

I climbed the overgrown hill pretty easily, even though it was really hard to see. My eyes had adjusted for the most part, and I'd done this so many times with Tom that I was used to it. But I noticed something in the distance. There was a light.

A rush of excitement warmed my insides for the first time in days. Why hadn't I come here sooner?

There were never any lights up here. Usually, I had a flashlight with me to see. I hoped that there would still be one at the cabin, but this light was coming from somewhere *near* the cabin.

Could it be? No ... it couldn't, could it?

Was Tom waiting here for me all along?

I quickened my pace, needing to know where the light was coming from. As I climbed, bugs flew all around, attacking me. I swatted at the mosquitos that were trying to get me to turn back, hoping they'd let me be. But it seemed to only instigate them and they attacked me more.

"Leave me alone," I called out with a massive air swat that missed every mosquito around me.

The light got brighter and brighter, and finally, I was able to see where it was coming from ... a tree. I stopped and stared at it, then looked at the abandoned cabin that Tom and I always went to.

I was within twenty yards of the tree.

Slowly, I walked up to the tree and touched it. A rush of heat warmed my fingertips while I traced the bark all around the light, until I located a carving mid-way up: *a space shuttle.* I rubbed the outline of it and my mind flashbacked to the day that Tom and I had etched that into the tree.

Tom had come prepared on a hot summer day with his dad's pocket knife. He brought it, knowing that we had been trying to leave our mark on this tree many times, but none of the tree branches on the ground were strong enough to make a lasting imprint.

He took the knife to the tree and began carving. I let him make the first cut because he brought the knife. "Which planet would you want to go to first?" I had asked, carefully watching the shape that he was carving.

"I dunno. I mean any of them would be cool to me. You're the picky one!" We both shared a laugh. "Besides, I'll probably be waiting in the spaceship until you explore the area!" Tom leaned back and looked at the shape of the nose for the shuttle and nodded with approval. Then he passed the knife to me.

I added more details and started engraving the left wing. "Left side!" I called out.

"Your favorite ... you always go left for some reason."

Just like at Space Camp, where for the past three years I took the left seat in the simulator with Tom. "It's the best way to go!" I said.

"Lucky for us, I'll be flying that space shuttle because I'm sure we'll need to make a right at some point!"

"Man, I can't wait to explore space with you, buddy!" I handed Tom back the knife and he drew in the right side of the ship.

That had been it.

I stepped back from the tree, into reality, and looked at the cool engraving. My hand ran its course over the right wing of the shuttle and back to the top. That had been such a great day.

I looked farther up the tree and the light was still shining—through it. This was our tree. The light couldn't be a coincidence … could it?

Cautiously, I climbed a branch to get higher and see what this light was. *Crack!* Branches fell down around me as I kept pulling myself up until I reached the light. I popped my head up and could see directly *through* the tree. A perfect circle had been expertly extracted from the trunk of the tree and there was a bright light inside of it. I wiggled around and tried to see from the other side of the tree what the light looked like, and it was the same. The light was *inside* the tree.

Should I reach in there?

Slowly, I put my left hand out, wincing as I got closer and closer to the hole. First, I touched the bark surrounding the hole and then guided my hand to go into it. I braced myself, ready to touch it, but when I finally reached out my hand, it didn't go through. It was blocked, as if an invisible piece of glass surrounded the outside of the hole.

I punched my hand into the middle, but nothing happened. It didn't move in any way, but it hurt my hand to the point where I had to shake it out.

What the—?

I maneuvered around to the other side of the hole to try to see if I could get into the tree that way and find out what that light was. But the same thing happened. *Who would have put a piece of glass or plexiglass inside this tree?*

Instinctively, I reached both of my hands out and touched the tree, then I brought my face closer to the hole. Would I be able to see anything if I put my face into it?

My heart started beating faster, making me a little anxious. Would something happen to me if I looked deep inside the tree?

I took a deep breath.

Slowly, I closed my right eye and brought my left eye to the hole.

The light was so bright that it made me squint.

A dark shadow was off in the distance moving closer and closer to my eye. It was coming toward me!

My heart pounded in my chest as it came closer and closer. It was about to reach the hole, so I jumped back, without waiting to see what it was.

CHAPTER TWO

I jumped up from my bed, nearly crashing to the ground. It was all a nightmare, but it had felt so real. Everything about it—even the vision within the dream.

I rubbed my forehead as I thought long and hard about what the dream could have meant. Tom had to be waiting at the cabin. Didn't he?

But what was that light? Would the light be there at the abandoned cabin where Tom and I had spent so many days discussing our future space plans? There was one way to find out, but I needed someone to go with me, just in case.

Loud voices from downstairs interrupted my thoughts. My parents were talking about something with my big brother. That was it. Joel. He had come home from college for Tom's funeral. He would listen to me. He'd believe me, but I would have to tell him everything first.

*   *   *

I packed my duffle bag with clothes, a sleeping bag, a few flashlights, and some other random supplies that I thought I might need—including the space shuttle model that Tom was trying to bring back to me—the one that caused his accident.

Joel waited downstairs for me. We told our parents that we were going to be staying at his apartment near college for the night. We knew that they would never be okay with us spending the night in an abandoned cabin in the woods, so we kept that between us.

It gave me chills thinking about it, but deep in my heart, I thought that Tom was going to be there. There had to be a reason why I had that dream—why it felt so real and important to go to the cabin.

I rushed downstairs and could hear my mom say to Joel, "I hope this helps."

He nodded to her and then looked at me. "Ready to go?"

I put a smile on my face, at least for now, and let out a, "Yeah!" That was the most positive emotion I had shown them in days.

Both of my parents swooped in and gave me a bear hug. "Keep him safe," my dad said as he pulled away. He dug into his pocket and pulled out a twenty-dollar bill, then handed it to Joel. "Get some pizza or something on us."

Joel thanked him and opened the door, leading me out. I ran to his car and threw my duffle bag in the back seat. I got into the front; it was time to go. My brother got into the driver's side and together we looked back at the house and waved. He started the car. "You really think we're going to find him, don't you?"

"Yeah … I do."

And with that, we headed to the cabin.

The sky darkened quickly during our ride. It wasn't a far drive—by bike, it took forever, but by car it was only about ten minutes.

I kept staring out the window. In my head, I could see Tom sitting on a rock outside of the cabin waiting for me. "What took you so long?" he'd ask.

I'd charge toward him and we'd do our secret handshake—a light kick to the shin, an elbow tap, two fist pumps on our own fist, then a pat on the back. *Ah man, what I wouldn't give to do our shake one more time,* I thought. I hoped that this trip would give me that chance.

The window went down and cold air blew across my face. I looked toward my brother.

"Hey! I was talking to you!" he said, while rolling the window back up.

"Sorry, I was spacing out."

"I noticed." Joel turned down a side street. "You're gonna have to tell me how to get there once I get off the main road."

"Okay." My head instinctively turned back to the window.

"Hey…" Joel waited for me to look back at him. "Don't let this get you down more if you don't find him here. Use this time to make your peace with everything, whether you see him or not."

I nodded and turned back to the window, unsure of how I felt about that statement.

"Next left," I said. "Then one more left."

"Couldn't we have turned a street before and it would've been on the right?"

"No. Always left."

Before long, we were there. I opened the car door and stared up the dark, grassy hill from my nightmare or dream, whatever it was. Something was different. Tom was there. I could tell.

I rushed to the back seat and opened my bag. I pulled out the flashlight and turned it on, then I shined it up the hill.

"3, 2, 1 … blastoff!" I quietly mouthed to myself, then charged up the hill as fast as I could.

"Whoa! Wait up!" Joel called out.

I didn't turn back, my legs kept churning, climbing. I moved the flashlight all around, trying to see if there was anything out of the ordinary, but there wasn't. Yet.

Finally, the flashlight reached a large tree— *the* large tree—from my dream.

I stopped dead in my tracks and examined it from afar. A rush of adrenaline swooped through my body, making me feel like I might pass out.

I took a step closer.

Then another.

And another.

I stood in front of the tree. I moved the flashlight all around until I found the space shuttle that we had engraved.

I put my fingers out and touched the engraving, pressing my palm to it. My hand covered the space shuttle. That was it. Desperately, my eyes searched for the light from my dream, but the tree was completely normal. I climbed up one branch so that I could see if there was a hole cut into the tree. My feet struggled to hold my balance as the tree branch felt weak.

There wasn't a hole in the center or a weird light anywhere. Nothing.

I moved the flashlight toward the cabin, which was very close by.

Creeeeaaaaaaaakkkkkkkkk ... Slammmmmmmm ...
Creeeeaaaaaaaakkkkkkkkk ... Slammmmmmmm ...

Every muscle in my body tightened as I flinched. The branch that I was standing on snapped because of my sharp movement. I fell backward. Luckily, Joel was there to catch me. "Gotcha," he groaned, letting me down easily.

"Did you hear that?" I asked.

He nodded and pointed his light to the cabin. "It's coming from there." His voice cracked.

Creeeeaaaaaaaakkkkkkkkk ... Slammmmmmmm ...

My stomach was in knots. Everything was weird.

I looked harder toward the cabin. Joel pointed.

It was the door.

Opening, then closing.

Creeeeaaaaaaaakkkkkkkkk ... Slammmmmmmm ...

The sound was ... purposeful. Who or what was doing that?

CHAPTER THREE

Joel pulled me behind him, blocking anything that might charge at us. He led the way with his flashlight as we moved closer to the cabin.

"Do you think it's Tom?" I whispered from behind him—my mind was in a twist, like a pretzel. Sure, I had hoped that Tom was there, but did I really think that he would be waiting inside the cabin? I don't know.

"It's something." Joel quietly kept moving forward. He didn't waiver. Step by step, we got closer and closer to the cabin until we stood in front of it.

The door was open.

I took a step out from behind him and then took one step closer to the cabin and tried to shine the flashlight inside. But just as the light touched the cabin's side wall, the door slammed shut again.

I cringed. My insides were doing somersaults. Joel's and my eyes met. He looked as scared as me.

Together we stepped onto the wooden platform. The floorboards moaned as if they struggled to hold us both. Joel took another step and *crunch!* One of the boards snapped. "Are you sure this is safe?" he asked, while I stumbled into him, almost knocking him over.

"Shhhhh!" I reached out to the door and grabbed the brass handle.

The cabin was small, made of dark wood with two large, cracked rectangular windows. That was how Tom and I had first gotten into this place. The door was always shut, but we climbed in through the window. The first time we got inside, we could see that the place was old and abandoned. We always wondered who built the cabin. Perhaps it was made by beings from space who knew we would find it and set up our headquarters here. Tom and I made this place our command center—our Houston.

Joel shined his flashlight on the door where there were really deep scratches dug into the wood. It looked like a bear claw had gone through it and the scratches looked fresh. "Recognize these?" he asked.

"No." I gulped.

I shook off the recent fears that had entered my mind. My search was bigger than all of that. I had to know if Tom was inside. I pulled the handle.

Squuuuuueeeeeeaaaaaakkkkkkk! The door screeched as it opened and something inside the cabin shuffled across the ground, away from us. Quickly, we shined our lights to follow the sound. Leaves and brush flew into the air. Something or someone else was there.

I almost let out a scream.

"You sure you want to do this?" Joel asked.

I nodded and we took a step inside. The cabin wasn't big enough for someone to hide, so at any moment they or it was going to come into view.

There was nothing.

Slowly, we walked to the other side of the cabin and to the back door. There was a small wooden deck off the back. We pushed open the door.

Creaaaakkkkk!

The two rocking chairs on the deck were moving.

I pointed and Joel led the way out there. "Who's here?" he yelled, jumping out to confront whoever was sitting in the chair.

"Yeah, who is it ..." I started to say, following him, but I realized that no one was there.

"The wind," Joel said. "It has to be the wind."

It didn't feel that windy out, but that had to be the reason for all of this movement because no one was there.

Something rustled behind us, inside the cabin. Joel jerked his flashlight around and toward the sound. He pulled open the back door.

A mouse scurried toward the front door.

I exhaled. "Phhhhewwww! I really thought there was something here."

Joel let out a laugh as the tension left the cabin with the rodent. He went toward the front of the cabin and opened the door so the mouse could run out. "We're alone now."

I turned back to the rocking chairs and sat in the one on the left—my chair. Joel sat in the other one and we both looked to the sky.

It was pitch black out. However, the stars lit up the sky—it was amazing! This view always reminded me how much I wanted to be in space. There were a gazillion stars in the sky. I could make out constellation after constellation. First, Orion's belt, then the Big and Little Dippers. The North Star. I could even see Mars. It was a beautiful night. "Wow, Tom would've loved this." I searched the sky, constantly finding more breathtaking sights.

"Yeah, wow. Beautiful night," Joel said, as he stretched out his legs, then his neck. "So you really want to go up there, huh?"

"It's my dream. Our dream. Tom and I were supposed to do it together. But not anymore." Thoughts of Space Camp, the simulator, and the space shuttle toy that caused Tom's accident filled my head. Every day I wished that I could go back in time and grab that space shuttle from his bag.

"You can still do it," Joel said, staring at me. "Don't take that dream away from yourself. Tom wouldn't want you to do that."

"I know. But I hate that it was my fault," I said, clenching my lips tightly together, trying to hold back tears.

"Stop it," Joel said, sitting up straight. "That's not true."

"If I hadn't left that stupid space shuttle—"

Before I could finish, Joel interrupted me. "That stupid space shuttle is why you two were best friends."

"We were supposed to do all of it together, though. It's not fair!"

"I know it's not. But he'll always be with you, every step of the way,"

"Where is he? I don't see him," I raised my voice. "That's the only reason why we're here—because I thought Tom would be here. I can't believe he would just leave me. Aughhhhhhhhh!"

I lost it. I screamed and kept screaming. I was so angry and disappointed. My vocal cords tightened, wanting to snap from the intense rage that was leaving my body. I really thought that I could find Tom at the cabin and solve everything. I guess I was wrong.

Joel reached out and patted me on the back. "I'm sure he's looking for you, too. Your paths haven't crossed again yet. Whether it happens tonight or not, he'll find you."

"Do you really believe that?" I tried calming myself down.

"There's no way he's just gone. He may've left this world, but there are other realms and at some point, you'll find a way there. But you have to promise me one thing." Joel said, holding his pointer finger in the air.

"What?"

"That *you* come back."

I scrunched my face as a warm tear or two fell down my cheeks.

"Because I don't want to go through what you're going through right now."

I nodded, sniffing back my emotions. "Thanks, Joel." I looked off into the woods. "I'm going to wander around for a minute, but I'll be back."

He started to get up out of the rocker and said, "Do you want company?"

"No, it's okay, keep an eye out here." I shined my flashlight on the forest around the back of the cabin. I stepped off the deck and walked around the area.

I ventured through the grassy woods and found myself back at the tree. Still, there was no circle or hole in it with light streaming through it. What had that dream meant?

"Tom!" I yelled as loud as I could. There was silence, except the haunting echo of my call. "Tom!" I yelled out again. "Where are you?"

My words repeated back to me.

I wandered a little deeper into the woods without going too far. There was nothing. It was so quiet—eerily quiet. Other than me yelling and stomping around, it seemed that there wasn't anyone else alive in these woods.

Feeling defeated, I turned around and walked back to the cabin. I followed the beam of my flashlight to the back deck. I wondered if Joel had seen anything. "Joel," I called out.

There was no answer.

I started to yell his name again, until I saw him passed out in the rocking chair. I smiled, knowing how much I appreciated him being here. Then I walked around to the front of the cabin and opened the door. My duffle bag was on the ground and instead of waking Joel, I pulled out my sleeping bag and set it up on the floor in the main part of the cabin.

I couldn't help but sigh with frustration when I got into it. This was all a waste. Tom wasn't here. Why had I thought he was going to be? Was he supposed to just be sitting on the ground, waiting for me? Come on, why had I thought that? A few more tears fell down my face.

Ugh, this was my new normal, I thought.

I lay in my sleeping bag, gazing off—almost meditative—listening to the faint, distant sounds of the forest. Crickets quietly chirped, mosquitos buzzed in the distance, and an owl hooted. It was all somewhat soothing.

Maybe this was what I needed. My eyelids got heavy. One eye closed, while the other one hung on, trying to stay awake and keep watch for anything out of the ordinary. Moments later, the other one closed.

I was out cold until a rumble and a loud thud shook the cabin.

CHAPTER FOUR

I shot up from my sleeping bag. My heart pounded in my chest. Chills raced up my spine. My eyes darted around the cabin. *What was that?* I thought.

Desperately, I reached for my flashlight, but it was so dark I couldn't find it. My hands frantically felt everywhere nearby, until finally, I located it. I clicked the button, but it wouldn't turn on. Augh! Why hadn't I brought more batteries?

I looked at my watch and lit up the sides of it, so I could see the time: 2:15 a.m.

Had I been dreaming? Again?

I listened closely. Silence.

I shook off the scare and settled back into my sleeping bag. I rolled around a few times, trying to get comfortable. My body was still tight and on edge, prepared for anything.

"Matty …"

I swore someone said my name.

Painful spikes of ice shot through my entire body. Was someone here? Was it Joel? It had to be him.

I slipped out of the sleeping bag and cautiously walked toward the door that led to the back deck. Slowly, I opened it, "Joel." I whispered loudly, peering out. I expected to see him awake and trying to get my attention. "Joel," my voice cracked … why wasn't he answering?

I got to the deck with my back holding the door ajar. Lucky for me, the moon was bright, so I was able to see Joel. He wasn't awake. Instead, he was still sound asleep in the chair.

If he was sleeping, who had said my name?

Boooooommmmm! A loud sound shook the cabin again. It sounded like an elephant jumped on the boards at the entrance. My neck swung around as my eyes were drawn to the front door.

It was shaking.

Someone or something was trying to get inside.

"Joel!" I whispered, shaking his shoulder.

Drool fell from his mouth as he mumbled something and rolled over.

Boooooommmm! Another step. How could Joel not hear that?

Crunch! The boards sounded like they were being destroyed.

I couldn't even imagine what was outside that door.

Cold sensations shot up my spine, while my legs twitched. I looked back at Joel and tried one more time to wake him, but it wasn't happening. And then, a light in the shape of a circle entered the cabin … through the door. I tried to focus on it, but it was so bright. My hands shielded my face, while my eyes slowly adjusted to the light that was coming from a peephole in the door.

I had never noticed a peephole before.

I stepped back inside the cabin, letting the deck door close. Was it Tom?

"Tom," I whispered.

My voice echoed back again, much like how it did in the woods.

"Tom … is that you?"

Still nothing but my own voice coming back at me.

I shook out my chills and got close to the door. Footsteps and wood crunching were still happening, but I couldn't tell if the sounds were farther off in the woods or right outside.

I took one more step. Wait.

I stopped. What was I doing? Wouldn't Tom have answered by now? Would he really be trying to scare me?

It couldn't be him.

But that light was drawing me in as if it were a magnet. I swore that I had heard a voice again, but it wasn't saying anything—it sounded like weird, gargling noises. That could have been anything though, like maybe my stomach?

I stood still at the door. Something was on the other side of it—I could hear them breathing. I was terrified, but I knew there were only two ways to find out what was there. I had to either open the door or look through the newly formed peephole.

My hand reached out for the door. I was about to open it. Instead, my hands shifted to the door frame and I brought my eye closer to the door. I raised myself on my tippy toes. I was about to do it … I was going to look through the peephole.

But then I didn't. I couldn't. My hand dropped to the door handle and I turned it.

I really hoped that Tom was on the other side, waiting for me.

CHAPTER FIVE

I slowly craned my head around the wooden door, but there was nothing.

I stepped out onto the front deck, which caused another loud creak, much like what I had just been hearing. I looked off into the dark woods. The light that shot through the peephole of the cabin was gone and I couldn't see anyone or anything. It was dead silent. There was no movement whatsoever; even the night breeze seemed to stop completely. The trees stood tall and the leaves hung in place. Nothing was disturbed.

I went back inside the cabin and closed the door. I stopped and stared at it. Something was different. There was no peephole.

What the—? How is that possible? I thought.

My emotions flooded my brain. I was scared. I was angry. Maybe finding Tom was all a pipe dream. Was it really possible? At this point, it seemed like it was never going to happen.

I felt defeated. Since the light from outside was gone, I walked back toward my sleeping bag. Before I could lay down, the light came back. It shined into the cabin ... through the peephole. Goosebumps raced to the surface of my skin. My face boiled with fear.

There was something really weird going on.

The peephole once again captivated my attention. It was the only light throughout the center of the cabin. It was eerie and mysterious, looking like it led to somewhere else — somewhere different than outside of the cabin.

Was Tom there this time? Was he trying to communicate with me? I was convincing myself that it had to be Tom. I turned back to the door and again took a step towards it. The floor creaked as I tiptoed through the main area, step by step, trying not to make any extra noises. I rested my hands against the door. I put my ear to it and listened.

Crash! Something hit the door, forcing my head back away from the wood. What was going on? I shrugged off the mild pain in my head — I was basically in shock. There *was* definitely something on the other side of the door.

I closed my eyes and took a deep breath, trying to ease my erratic gasping. Slowly, I got onto my tippy toes and lifted my neck to the peephole. My heart pounded in my chest—so much so that I felt lightheaded.

Steadying myself, I took another deep breath.

I looked into the light from the peephole—it was blinding. Slowly, the light dimmed until there was nothing! The light was gone. It was pitch black through the peephole.

I pulled my head back and looked at the door.

The light came rushing through the cabin again like a laser beam, nearly splitting the place in two.

Quickly, I got back onto my tippy toes and again pressed my eye against the peephole. This time there was something there.

CHAPTER SIX

I blinked my eye, trying to focus on what I was looking at. I scrunched my face and squinted, until I finally realized what was on the other side of the peephole.

An eye was staring back at me.

This wasn't just any eye—a thin, yellow, lizard-like eye had me frozen in place. I used all of my might to try and close my own eye, but I couldn't. More of the yellow eye came into focus. I could make out every blood vessel, the diameter of its pupil, and the whiteness around the outside of this eye. All of this was so freaky, so strange.

Whose eye was I looking at? And why wasn't it blinking? Even worse than that, if I could make out every detail of their eye, could they do the same with mine? Something about all of this felt out of this world, as if it wasn't real—a dream. Yes, it had to be a dream.

I used my left hand to pinch myself. Ouch! It actually hurt. I tried using my hands to push away from the door, to remove myself from the peephole, but I couldn't. I was magnetized to the spot.

I tried to yell for my brother, but my voice didn't work. If this wasn't a dream ... or a nightmare, something really strange was happening in the woods. And if it was the second, I really hoped that it had something to do with Tom.

"Tom," I tried to call out, but his name only sounded in my head. Nothing came out of my mouth.

The eye looking into mine wasn't Tom's. So, whose was it?

The quiet was eerie. Whatever was on the other side of this door was standing deadly still. It didn't even sound like they were breathing. Meanwhile, I was panting like crazy but even my heavy breathing didn't make a sound. Everything around me had gone quiet.

Part of me really wanted this eye to react, to do something so that I knew that it saw me. But the other part of me hoped that I was invisible to it and whatever was standing out there would vanish without a trace.

My hands were still pressed against the door, pushing to try and get away ... until, that was, my fingers started tingling. A feeling like you get from touching a hot wire rushed up my arms and stopped before reaching my face. Tingling sensations rushed down my chest, into my legs. Sparks attacked my body, disconnecting it from reality, as if my brain no longer worked with the rest of me.

The sensations turned into a numbing feeling. My peripheral vision was fading to black. I had tunnel vision—the only thing I could see was that eye.

I tried to yell again for my brother, but my mouth didn't respond the way it was supposed to. I convulsed like I was holding back a dry heave. My left shoulder shook, then my right. My whole body was giving out, yet I was still standing at the peephole.

My vision closed in even more. Things were getting dark. The eye through the peephole shrunk. My stare was still unbreakable, until the yellow eye closed and everything went black.

CHAPTER SEVEN

I heard something click in place and the air around me changed. I reached out. I was in something—it felt like a tube of sorts … wait, was this a coffin?

Everything started spinning. Slowly at first, then it picked up speed little by little, until I was moving at hyperspeed. Bright, color-changing lights flashed all around me.

I opened my eyes, but I couldn't see anything, only colors speeding past me, making it seem like I was going at the speed of light. It was nauseating. I shielded my eyes, while my hands reached all around, desperate to feel what I was inside of. The structure felt hard, but I couldn't tell if it was made of glass, metal, or something else. I was surrounded by whatever this was.

How did I get put into this thing? I thought.

It went faster and faster, until the colors mixed together and everything turned black again. Had I suddenly gone blind?

How was I going to get out of it? I had never been claustrophobic in my life, but the tube ... the thing I was in was certainly challenging my feelings about tight spaces. I attempted to move around to try and break out of it. I slid to the bottom of it, hoping there would be an exit hatch, similar to what a space pod would have. No luck. There wasn't anything that could open it up. I propelled myself off the bottom with my legs and tried reaching for the same thing at the top. Still nothing. The tube angled downward a little more and it spun out of control, even faster. I closed my eyes and hoped for the best. Was this it for me? Was I dying?

My stomach roared and instantly, it felt like I could puke at any moment. *Come on, stop! This has to stop!* I thought.

A sound of a door opening filled the silence. Gusts of air hit me in the face. The top of the tube had ripped off. Small lights filled the air, like stars. The tube, or half-tube by then, had paused in midair. I watched as those stars raced across the sky like a meteor shower.

The tube started spinning again, so fast that it pressed me against the bottom half that was still there. It was so dizzying. Like being in the Multi-Axis Trainer at Space Camp. My neck couldn't watch the stars anymore. My head leaned back. I had given up. My eyes couldn't focus anymore.

The spinning stopped and the tube shifted upright. The floor gave out and I dropped, freefalling.

I tried to scream, but I couldn't. My stomach rushed through my throat, attempting to escape my body as I raced through the air at the speed of light.

I kept falling.

And falling.

Was I ever going to land?

CHAPTER EIGHT

Thud!

Finally, I hit the ground. It should have hurt, but it didn't.

How had I fallen that far and crashed into the ground without a scratch?

I was comfortably sitting in wet, dewy grass. I wiggled my hands and feet, and pinched my arms to make sure that they weren't numb anymore. Ouch! They definitely weren't—the pinching still hurt.

The distant moon brought enough light for me to be able to see again, at least enough to look around the area. I was in the woods. Similar to the woods where the cabin was, but different.

There was a large tree here as well. I walked over to it and inspected it. I had a sinking feeling that this was *the* tree from outside the cabin. My hands reached up to locate the space shuttle etching, but I couldn't find it. My fingers did another lap across the bark of the tree. When I got back to where the engraving was supposed to be, there was something. I could feel a part of the space shuttle—the lines that made its outer edges.

Then I felt for more of it.

Whoa! I jumped back. The space shuttle that Tom and I had etched into the tree by the cabin was being engraved into the tree in front of me … as I stood there. How?

All of a sudden, I had a terrible pain in my stomach. A rush of fluid stormed up through my body and reached my throat. I couldn't keep it inside. I puked everywhere.

My body was weak. I strained to lift my head up and call for my brother, but no sound came out of my mouth. Instead, my voice echoed in my own head, trapped inside me. The word "Joel" caused pulsating sensations inside my brain. This was like nothing I'd ever felt before. And boy was it painful—so much so that my eyes squinted and I threw my head into the ground, hoping that it would stop throbbing.

"Aughhhhhhhh!" I tried to scream, but the effort only made the pain worse. Not only did the scream not come out of me, it caused a drum-like reaction in my head. Or worse yet, like someone smashed cymbals between my ears. I collapsed to the ground, panting until I was basically out of breath. My eyes didn't want to open. They were wet with tears as my body adjusted to wherever I was, and from whatever I had been through.

Slowly, I began to pick myself up in a sort of push-up position and was able to look around. There was the cabin—the one that Joel and I were sleeping at.

I must've really been having a nightmare.

I got up to my feet and walked toward the cabin. Perhaps if I went inside, I could end this nightmare and be back asleep. I stomped onto the front deck, hoping that it would cause a loud noise that would wake me up. But there was no sound. Just get inside … that was the plan anyway, but the door handle was gone. Gone.

I pushed against the door. Nothing happened. It wouldn't budge. I tried to yell for Joel, already forgetting about the pain that happened the last time I yelled. Once again, it attacked my skull. A horrible, sharp pain.

Panic overcame the rest of my body and more fluid shot out of me. My body collapsed, frozen in place on the porch. From the ground, I reached my ice-cold hand up to the door again, but there was still no handle.

Then I noticed the peephole. It was there—if I looked through it, maybe it would send me back inside. The opposite of what had just happened to me. I could try. It took everything inside of me to get back up and press my eye to the peephole. The view was blurry and I couldn't see anything inside.

An even fiercer, intense pain shot through my entire body. I screamed uncontrollably. Nothing came out. I tried again. I slammed my eyes shut and clenched my jaw. Instinctively, I clawed at the door, leaving fresh etchings in the wood. I hoped that my brother would hear my clawing and open the door.

Why was nothing happening? I thought.

I heard a rumbling in the distance, deep in the woods.

The sound got louder.

Trees swayed back and forth as the whole area shook.

Someone or something was coming for me.

CHAPTER NINE

I could barely move. I looked around, desperate to find somewhere to hide as the sounds were getting closer. There was nowhere. Whatever was coming for me would be there any minute. I hoped that Tom was behind it all ... somehow. I slumped onto the floorboards of the porch.

The shadow of a person slowly came into view from the woods. They stopped and faced me. They were looking at me. I couldn't tell who it was. But it didn't appear to be Tom.

Butterflies filled my stomach and dreadful thoughts entered my head. Maybe this wasn't a nightmare after all. Could I be dead already? Or about to die? Maybe Tom never died ... maybe I was the one who did.

The person came out of the woods and methodically approached me. They were very deliberate with their steps. A thick fog seemed to be floating behind them—keeping pace with them. The person kept moving until they stepped close enough for me to see clearly. It was a young girl. She looked to be about my age. She had strawberry blonde hair and a face full of freckles. Her arms and legs were like toothpicks. She wore big, silver framed glasses that hid most of her face.

Why was I scared of that person?

Forget that. I wasn't going to sit there and be scared of a girl my age. I tried to get to my feet.

She raised her arm and my whole body became paralyzed.

Whoa!

"Sit," I heard in my head, but it wasn't said out loud. My head spun, looking back and forth. I widened my eyes to look closer at her. She was wearing a purple cape that was tightly secured around her neck. It draped behind her as she walked. She dragged a large, black walking stick that appeared to be a staff on the ground next to her. It was nearly as tall as she was.

The girl stared around the area and looked down at me. She reached up to her glasses and took them off. Gently, she put them inside the pocket of the cape and lightly tapped the pocket where she'd inserted them. Slowly, she looked up, showing off her bright yellow, lizard-like eyes.

Chills raced up my spine. Was it her eye that had stared back at me through the peephole?

I was hypnotized.

"Hello," I tried to say, but I was still unable to talk. The pain from trying to speak broke my stare.

She raised her arm again, motioning for me to be still. My body didn't give me a choice. It remained at rest and waited for her to say more.

She walked closer to me. Her steps continued to be methodical and slow.

Was this girl responsible for all that happened? That coffin tube that flew through the air? The sounds in the woods? Was all of that because of her? My mind raced.

Who was she and what was she doing here … at the cabin?

Emphatically, she raised her arm. My mind went blank. Everything was completely still. It was as if she could sense my questions.

The girl circled me. My head followed her movement. She stopped in front of me after doing a full 360 degrees. Finally, I heard her sweet voice. "I will answer your questions, but only for a moment," she said. "Time's wasting. You are the new Peephole Master."

CHAPTER TEN

I sat there, helpless, on the verge of a panic attack. The concept of being in outer space never scared me, but this girl terrified me. She had a power unlike any that I had ever seen before.

What was she talking about ... Peephole Master? Was she joking?

I couldn't speak, but my thoughts raced. *Who is this girl? What is she doing here? Why me? What is happening?*

Each time those questions filled my head, she raised her arm. Immediately, all of my thoughts disappeared, like she was using some sort of twisted magic. The girl sat down in front of me, cross-legged, on the small porch. The faint light from the pale moonlight backlit her, adding a glow around her body. "You have freed me. Thank you."

I still couldn't talk. But I wasn't really sure if I should say you're welcome or not. *Freed her … from what? How?*

"You will figure out why you were chosen. I assure you of that. Sometimes that takes time, but keep in mind that you don't have an unlimited amount of time, especially if you want to make it back to the other side."

The other side? Which side was I on now?

"This is the In-Between."

The girl pointed at the peephole on the outside of the cabin. "That peephole is a gateway to this side. Spirits can come and go in between finding their destinies. Most of them are lost, which is where you come in."

She paused and stared at me. I think she was waiting for me to give her more of a reaction. I was in shock though—my face had to be as pale as a ghost. "You are a lost, *living* soul. In order to get your life back, you'll have to help a spirit get over their issue, whatever it may be. Only you will know what that is. You've been chosen based on which spirit is next to seek help."

Me? Help a spirit? How is that possible?

"Only you will be able to understand them. They won't be able to talk or communicate in the traditional sense, but you'll be able to hear

46

them like I can hear you. They don't always know why they're lost. You have to figure that out."

The girl was very calm. She breathed slowly, then continued. "You will use your powers as the Peephole Master. These glasses …" She reached into the cape pocket and flashed them at me. "They allow you to see things others can't. You can go places others won't be able to go. And this walking stick …" She tapped the stick on the ground. "It will allow you to create noise in the real world. And your touch …" She came over to me and touched my shoulder.

Instantly, we were transported to a dark area with lots of small shining lights. It looked like outer space. "Your touch will take you to places deep inside others' minds. But you'll have to come back to the peephole at this cabin once you finish your mission, or you'll be stuck here. And one more thing, make sure you don't bring any of the Peephole Master items back to the real world with you. It could open another gateway."

My mind wasn't even working anymore. I could feel explosions going off in my head. None of what she told me seemed real or even possible.

Within another instant, she transported us from space and back to the deck of the log cabin.

We sat in front of each other in the same positions.

Why me?

"Your journey will take you to that answer. But be careful. There are also evil spirits in the In-Between who want to bring you to the Netherworld. Some of those spirits are powerful. They'll have powers similar to your own, stronger even, and they'll use deception and your own mind against you to try and bring you to the Netherworld. If you end up there, you'll *never* make it back to the real world." She paused. Her voice raised, "You can *never* get back from the Netherworld. Use all of your senses. Be strong."

Whoa … what if I can't do this?

"You have to, otherwise there's grave news. You will be lost in the In-Between until someone comes for you."

How long do I have?

"Time in the In-Between is different. You have the equivalent of one night in the real world, but that can seem like an eternity here."

How am I supposed to know how much time I have left?

"When you start losing the ability to communicate with your spirit, you have to finish your job."

Will there be a warning?

48

"Your powers will fade. You'll feel echoes within your head, and the cord around this cape ..." She grabbed the string that rested around her neck from the purple cape. "Will get tighter and tighter until it cuts off your airflow and takes away your voice."

She got up from the ground and started to remove the cape. "This is your responsibility now."

Wait! How will I know if I helped the spirit or not?

"You'll know. But keep in mind, the journey isn't only about the other being. It's about you, too. I hope you find what you're looking for."

What does that mean? My best friend Tom?

"The Tom you ask about is in the In-Between, but focus on the spirit you have to help. Otherwise, you too could be trapped. You have everything you need. Once I give you this cape, you will assume your duties as the new Peephole Master."

No! Wait…. How do I find Tom?

"See you on the other side, Matty."

Before I could ask her how she knew my name, the girl tossed the cape in the air at me, and she was gone.

CHAPTER ELEVEN

"Noooooooooooo!" I yelled as loud as I could. At first the sound was lost inside my head, causing a sharp pain that made me want to rip my skull in half.

When the cape landed on me, my scream became audible and the decibel level shook the forest.

The purple cape covered me the same way that an oversized blanket would. But, as I shifted around and adjusted, so did the cape. It automatically fit itself to my body. The cape slid all the way up to my shoulders and the string reached out around my neck. The rest of it flowed down my back. I tried to fight it and get the cape off me, but there was nothing I could do.

Once it stopped altering its size, I made one last effort to rip it off me, but it didn't work. This was expertly tailored to me and there was no chance of me getting this off. I was going to have to figure out my mission and solve it. Or find Tom.

Suddenly, I could feel the powers of the cape entering my body. It was like a scalding hot rain showering over me, but it only lasted for a couple of seconds.

My body felt lighter. My senses were heightened. I felt somewhat invincible.

I paced back and forth on the porch, trying to get used to the way that my body felt. So much had happened in the past few minutes. I took it all in with a really deep breath and I let out a loud sigh. I could see wind coming from my breath! *Whoa! The trees shook because of my breath!*

My eyes darted to the walking stick. Slowly and methodically, I walked over and picked it up. More warm sensations rushed into my hands as I held it. I embraced the power and lifted the staff over my head, then smashed it into the ground.

Earthquake!

The cabin shook violently and so did all of the trees in the area. This must have been what caused the shaking before I got dragged into all of this. That girl must've been trying to reach me. Obviously, it had worked.

I'm not gonna lie, it was kind of cool to be this powerful. This had to be helpful in finding Tom, especially since I knew he was there. At least that was what she told me. Maybe she lied because she knew it would stop me from asking more questions. That thought caused rage to fill me. "Aughhhh!" I yelled out, smashing the walking stick into the ground again.

A loud boom went off in my head and a tree collapsed to the ground. I covered my eyes as branches soared through the air. When I opened them, I stared deep into the woods. There was a bright light in the distance, in the shape of a tube. That tube must have been how I got there.

I could hear something in my head, static almost, kind of like how it sounds when the radio communications went in and out on the spaceship.

Something else was in the woods.

"Hello … oh no, where am I?" A voice quivered and cracked, deep inside my head. It was different than someone talking out loud. This had to be what the girl was talking about.

I couldn't see the spirit yet, but it was in the area. My mission was about to begin.

CHAPTER TWELVE

"Hello?" I heard inside my head, followed by a painful groan. They must have been feeling what I did when I first got to the In-Between and couldn't talk out loud.

I gripped the walking stick and looked deeper into the woods, wondering who the spirit was going to be. It sounded like a man, older than me, maybe my dad's age? I couldn't tell yet. The light appeared to be fading in the distance. However, I could hear every blade of grass that was displaced as the person walked through the woods ... every mumble and breath was projected directly into my head.

What if the person was evil? What if they had done something really bad? Should I be concerned or scared of them?

The Peephole Master, or whatever she was, didn't prepare me for that.

I could sense the person's heavy breathing getting louder and closer. Another "Hello" filled my head. The person collapsed to the ground, still trying to talk out loud. In my head I heard, "No … what is happening?"

This was tough to take. Slowly and steadily, I walked toward the sounds. If I was going to find Tom or get back home, I had to face the spirit. Besides, it was a new adventure. Forget space, I was in the In-Between … and so was Tom!

I walked farther into the woods. Where was the person?

"Who's there?" I heard in my head, followed by another scream of pain. I stopped and looked around the area. Still nothing. I tightened the grip on my walking stick and slammed it into the ground, shaking the forest. Out of nowhere, a man … I think it was a man … jumped to his feet.

Who was this person? Could they somehow be connected to Tom? Would this spirit be the reason that I could see Tom again?

Was he … dead?

Questions filled my head as I got closer and closer to the man. The pace of his breathing rapidly increased. My senses were so enhanced.

The man smelled like a cold, wintery night, after fresh snow had fallen.

I could feel the man's body shaking in fear as I approached him slowly, the walking stick at my side.

One deep breath readied myself to meet this spirit—he was right in front of me. He looked up at me and I gasped. This was something I never expected to see.

In fact, I couldn't really see for that matter— well, I couldn't make out any details. I couldn't actually tell if the spirit was a man, or even a human being. It was just a red blur in front of me, in the shape of a human—sort of.

I walked around the red blur, getting close to it, but not yet touching it. All of my senses, except for my sight, were supercharged. My eyes couldn't focus. They couldn't see this spirit, or whatever it was. I squinted, tightening my face as much as I could, but it only made my sight worse. Why couldn't I see it?

My legs kept moving as I did another lap around this blur. *How could I help this thing if I couldn't even see it?* I thought.

Thoughts of the former Peephole Master entered my mind. Was this what she had seen when she looked at me?

I kept thinking on that, picturing the girl in my head.

No, there was something different about her. She had definitely been able to see me. ... The glasses!

I grabbed at the pocket of the cape. There they were, waiting for me to put them on, which I did.

I had never worn glasses before. My eyesight had always been perfect—great for astronauts! The weight of the silver frames on my face felt bulky, the shape didn't fit, they were way too big. But then, just like the cape, the glasses adjusted themselves until they fit perfectly.

Instantly, my vision was restored. The red blur wasn't just a color. It was a person—it was a man. He had a little bit of facial hair, not much—more than me, but I was only eleven! His hair was black and grey and very short—maybe falling out in the back. He was wearing a black, hooded sweatshirt and dark blue jeans. There really wasn't anything striking about his appearance.

The man looked up at me from his collapsed position with a terrified expression on his face. He tried to speak, but nothing came out of his mouth. Once again though, I heard him in my head. "Who are you?" He grabbed his throat in pain. "What's happening? Why can't I talk?" He was strong, fighting off the pain. He panted, begged almost—it was wearing him down. "Am I dead?" His voice trailed off.

I could feel this man freaking out, because I was experiencing it in my head. I wanted to dismiss all of this, the thoughts, the spirit—everything, so that I could find Tom. How was I going to help this person? What could I do for this guy? I wasn't even twelve years old yet.

I didn't want to be the stupid Peephole Master. Who would? I couldn't understand why I got stuck doing this. All I wanted was my best fr—. The string from the cape that was around my neck tightened up for a moment, reminding me of my job. Time was passing. The situation was real and I had to solve the mystery of why I had to help this man.

The spirit looked up at me, but before he could talk, I held the walking stick in one hand and raised the other, and everything fell quiet. "Relax. You are in the In-Between. I'm here to help you."

"How can you hear me?" the spirit struggled to ask, while looking up at me. Again, nothing came out audibly, but I heard it loud and clear.

I looked at the panic on this older man's face. I had never had power like this over anyone, let alone an adult. It made me feel like I was some kind of superhero. I stood tall and proud and announced, "I am the Peephole Master. But before I help you … where is Tom?" I asked.

"Who's Tom?" His response echoed through my brain.

CHAPTER THIRTEEN

I walked around the man, studying him. Was he telling the truth that he didn't know who Tom was? "What's your name?"

"John, Peephole Master." His voice cracked.

I stared at him. "You don't have to call me that. I'm Matty." I walked around him once more. "Why are you here?"

"I don't know."

"What's the last thing you remember?" There had to be something that connected us to each other. Perhaps his last memory was the key to all of this.

The man shrugged his shoulders with fear in his eyes.

I walked closer to him and touched his shoulder. Instantly, we were transported to a completely different area. Whoa! A quick dizzy spell jolted my body, but vanished. That was so fast.

The new area was very dark and we seemed to be inside a tunnel of sorts. I patted the metal walls around me as my eyes adjusted. John hung by my side. There was a very high ceiling, but I couldn't see the end of this tunnel ... it seemed to go on infinitely—it reminded me of a sewer.

I took a few steps in one direction. Nothing. I looked around, hoping that I could figure out where we were or what we should do next, but that wasn't clear. I stepped back in the other direction. Still nothing.

"Look!" John called out, pointing to something behind me.

Quickly, I turned around. A light in the shape of a circle on the wall had lit up. It wasn't there the minute before.

The circle was about eye level and about twenty or so feet away from us. I walked toward it, while John followed. The whole thing was really weird, but it felt like an adventure. Given how cool it was to transport here, I was interested to see what the circle did. I walked toward it.

When I got to it I put my hand out and pressed it like a button ... but nothing happened. The light from the circle was just bright enough to highlight a faint outline of a rectangle that appeared above the circle and floated all the way down to the ground—like a door. Was it another peephole?

There was no handle, so I wasn't really sure if this was a door, but I took a deep breath and put my left eye to the light. John stood behind me.

There was a family eating dinner at the table. "Strange," I said.

"What do you see?" John begged.

"There's a teenage boy, a mom, and a puppy. They're about to have dinner. The mom is pulling something out of the oven. It looks like a turkey," I said, realizing that I was able to be inside this room without my body.

I could go anywhere inside that peephole without physically being in the room.

"Ooh, turkey was my favorite. I could really go for some right now," John said, rubbing his stomach.

"I think they're waiting for someone. No one has anything on their plates yet." Seeing them reminded me of when my mom cooked and we were stuck waiting for my dad. "Maybe someone else is coming."

"Who?" John asked.

I leaned against the door, nearly dropping the walking stick. I grabbed hold of it, but pressed it hard into the ground.

The whole room rumbled. The family looked around in fear, as if they were trying to figure out where the noise was coming from. The mom got up and walked toward the door. She opened it. She was standing right in front of me. She looked me directly in the eyes. But she couldn't see me. The mom looked through me.

"What is it? What's going on?" John couldn't see her either.

"Hello?" the woman called out.

"Jessica?" John called out. "Are you there?" Frantically, he yelled again. Though, I was the only one who could hear him, inside my head.

I put my hand up to stop him from screaming more.

"She can't hear you," I said, wondering how he was able to hear her. How did he know her? "Who's Jessica?" She walked back to the table.

John dropped to the ground, as if he'd seen a ghost. He crawled to the door, but didn't know that the woman had slammed it shut. John did everything he could to get inside the room. He reached his hands up and clawed at the door. Exhausted, he said, "That was my wife."

"Oh," was all I could get out, along with a sigh.

I looked back into the peephole. A pit developed deep in my stomach—if anyone knew what it was like to lose someone it was me. But, this was the opposite of what I was going through—it was as if I was seeing it through Tom's eyes. *Yes, this is why I have to help John*, I thought at that moment. *He must be experiencing what Tom is experiencing. I have to see the other side of all of this.*

The phone rang and the woman got up to answer it. After listening to the voice on the other end, she collapsed to the ground. Her face looked the way I bet mine had when I found out about Tom.

My eyes burned as tears worked to flow out. Quickly, I reached up and wiped my face. "That's enough for now." I pulled my eye out of the peephole.

It was all terrible.

I looked at how upset John was. It made me think about Tom, which made me even more upset. Angry even. Ridiculous. Why was I part of John's story? I had enough. My hands squeezed the walking stick tight. Rage built up inside me. I didn't know what to do though. There was nowhere to go and the light from the peephole had disappeared like a candle flame in the wind.

I threw the walking stick to the corner. How was I supposed to help John? None of it made sense. He was hurting. I was hurting. I couldn't help him get over this ... who could?

I collapsed to the ground and sat with my back against the metal frame of the door, feeling sorry for myself. But before I could spend too much time wallowing, the cord around my neck tightened again.

CHAPTER FOURTEEN

"Arrrgggggghhhhhhhhhhhh!" I screamed as loud as I could. My throat was so dry that it tightened and cut off the end of my scream. Perhaps it could have also been because of the cord around my neck.

I looked at the man who I was supposed to help. He looked distraught—tucked against the wall, seemingly unable to move. Knowing that it was my job to figure out what to do, I slowly walked over to John and knelt down in front of him. He barely picked up his head.

"John is my dad's name," I said, hoping he'd offer more information about himself. There had to be a way to connect us. If I could figure out how to help him, it could lead me to Tom. Unfortunately, John remained silent and still. "Do you remember what happened?" I asked, even though I knew recalling details would probably be tough for him, if he remembered anything at all.

Surprisingly, John nodded and slightly looked up at me. "Some of it, then I woke up here."

I stared at him, desperate for more. But he didn't give me anything else. I knew what I had to do. My hand reached out and touched his shoulder. Again, we were transported to another area.

A different light shined before us. We both stared at it. John shot up, fully rejuvenated, and rushed over to the light from the newest peephole, beating me there. John put his eye to it. He yelled at me in his head. "Look at it! Tell me what you see."

I knew I had to check it out. I walked over to the peephole and put my eye to the bright circle, then looked through it.

Flames and smoke filled my line of sight. It was catastrophic.

"What do you see?" John repeatedly asked.

"Fire. Lots of it," I waited to see more.

The fire burned at a different house than the one from the previous peephole. Shelves crashed to the ground, furniture was upside down. The house was a disaster. I scoured the site. Pieces of mail flew through the air. I tried to make out the name on the envelopes as they went by, but the letters were distorted from the flames. I could, however, see the home address. It was only a couple of streets away from Tom's house.

Heat attacked my eyes and face as the house was being scorched. I coughed from the intense burning and smell of smoke. I grabbed my ears as I could hear a voice yelling from inside the house. Not just yelling, screaming.

I pulled my head away from the circle. "There's someone in the fire."

"Kevin," John said, as he put his head down in sorrow.

"Who's that?"

"My brother."

I pressed my eye back to the circle. Everything was happening at warp speed. No! A man collapsed on the bottom floor of the house. These powers of looking through the peephole were incredible. I was exploring *through* walls. I could see things that no one else would have been able to see. It was empowering, but everything I saw was also so sad.

Another person was searching for the body on the bottom level. It was a man. He yelled as loud as he could, calling out for Kevin. The man rushed through the burnt mess, struggling to make his way through the disaster. He dodged pieces of the ceiling as they fell to the ground. I could clearly see the path that the man had to take. I rooted for him, calling out directions, as if I could change what was happening in front of me.

"To your left!" I yelled, hoping to influence the man inside the room.

The man couldn't hear me. *The walking stick.* I thought. That was it, I could use it to cause sound in the real world.

But it was gone. I never picked it back up when I threw it and we were in the other area. I couldn't make any noise.

The man came into a clearer view as he got closer to Kevin in the bedroom. I could finally make out who it was. It was John.

John grabbed Kevin's lifeless body and put him on his back. He reversed course and climbed his way through the debris. It was a heroic act. The flames kept escalating, devouring the inside of the house. John struggled through the lower level and fell to the ground in exhaustion. Kevin toppled over John's motionless body and fell toward the front door.

An axe smashed through the door, and firefighters entered the house. First, they grabbed Kevin. He was closest to them.

Multiple firefighters grabbed hold of him and dragged Kevin out in time.

After successfully pulling him out, they went back in to check for more people. They could see John. I knew that they could see him because they yelled out to him. The firefighters were so close to him. One of them reached out and touched John's hand, but more wood cracked and fire busted through the ceiling, which crashed onto John.

"No!" the firefighter yelled.

Screams to get out came from outside the door. But the firefighter wouldn't give up. He ripped boards and pieces of rubble off of John. He was going to save him, until another fireman grabbed him. They pulled out the firefighter, leaving John to die. The man yelled and screamed for them to help John, but it was too late.

The rest of the roof collapsed and the entire house was engulfed in flames.

"Nooooooo!" I yelled, pulling my head away from this peephole.

John was dead.

I knew that I had to use what I saw to help John, but how? I wasn't sure what John was hanging onto. He had given his life to save his brother and left his own family behind. If anything, it was clear that I wasn't the only person who had lost someone.

John sat there on the ground, knowing what I had seen. Neither one of us said a word. Then, the peephole light went out.

Again, we were left alone in a pitch-black tunnel.

"You're ... dead?" I asked.

John didn't answer.

"You gave your life to save Kevin." I felt so bad for John.

"He's my brother. I had to. I would've done anything for him."

I acknowledged his heartfelt statement and thought about what I would do if I had been in John's situation. I probably would've done the same thing. "What happened before the fire?" I asked, trying to put the puzzle together. "Where were you?"

While John tried to think, my eyes were drawn back to the same peephole, as it lit up again. I jumped up, not waiting for John's response and looked through it once more, hoping for good news.

I still saw the burning house. I was able to move deeper into it and wander around. I approached a window and looked out, catching glimpses of more red, but it wasn't fire.

Before I could process what I was seeing, the dark area where we were standing violently rumbled. Thumping noises, similar to the ones that my staff made, surrounded us.

I pulled my head out of the peephole and my eyes shot up, trying to see something, but there was nothing.

I heard stomps—footsteps—and they got louder ... and louder.

CHAPTER FIFTEEN

John and I were pressed against the cold wall of the metal-like tunnel structure. The whole In-Between was cold ... dark ... and lonely. I had no idea what was coming toward us. But I really hoped that it would finally be something good.

Each step got louder and louder, but because of how dark and huge this space was, I had no idea where the steps were coming from. There wasn't a true echo that bounced off the walls here. Sounds got lost in this space, much like John and I were.

Suddenly, my senses went into overload. My ears perked up. My eyes watered. My nose picked up a scent—one that I was very familiar with. It was someone's body odor—not sweaty, gross, body odor, but a smell of someone who I knew. I couldn't tell if my heightened anxiety was alerting me to danger, or if I was excited.

"Do you feel that?" John communicated within my mind.

I knew what John was talking about. The area was filled with a wall of cold air. I didn't answer his question though, because I wasn't sure if whatever else was there would be able to hear me too.

Sounds of someone digging through a pant pocket came from nearby. Whatever it was, it was right next to us.

I could hear it breathe.

I cringed, tightening my back to the wall, unsure if I should try to communicate with this thing or not. Finally, the stress amplified and got the best of me. "Who goes there?" I yelled.

The rummaging through pockets stopped. There were sounds of cardboard pieces lightly rubbing together ... a scratch ... and a large spark transformed into fire.

Once again, the smell of smoke filled my nostrils. Was the whole tunnel on fire? Were we about to re-live what John had already experienced? Had those visions from before foreshadowed our demise?

"Relax, Matty!"

It wasn't in my head. It was out loud. My body tensed as my eyes tried to see anything through the smoke.

Slowly, the smoke disappeared and Tom stood in front of me.

"What?!" I yelled, excited to see my best friend.

Tom was wearing his bright blue Space Camp shirt and red sweatpants. It was similar to the outfit that he had been wearing when we left Space Camp. Tom had a smile from ear to ear on his face.

I figured it out. Somehow, I had accomplished what I came here to do and I was rewarded with seeing Tom. I knew I'd find him!

"Tom! No way!" I screeched with excitement.

A half smile appeared on his face.

Something seemed a little odd. Granted he just appeared, but things just didn't feel quite right yet. Maybe things were different in the In-Between and he didn't have all of his memories.

I was confused and surprisingly, unsure of what to do next. It felt like I had been waiting to see him again for so long that I was in shock. But, now, it was different than in the real world. Perhaps it was because we were in the In-Between, but part of me was skeptical about who this really was.

Still, I approached Tom and started our shake, but he stopped me and put a cigar in my mouth. I pushed it away and looked at the cigar still in Tom's hand. I was puzzled and stepped back from Tom. "You smoke now?"

"You have to here," Tom said, taking a puff. "It keeps the evil spirits away." Some of the ashes shook off the cigar and landed on his t-shirt, but he didn't seem to mind.

I reached out and wiped them away. "You always hated when your shirt got dirty."

"Yeah." Tom brushed at his shirt as well.

This was weird and so conflicting for me. I was looking at my best friend, but something didn't seem right. I couldn't help but analyze him. It all matched up—his face, his smile—it all seemed real—it had to be Tom. Why was I questioning him?

"Take a puff," Tom said, handing his cigar to me. "You don't want any evil spirits coming after you here, do you?"

No, I couldn't smoke. My parents would kill me if they knew about that. And why would I want to smoke? Yuck!

"You think I'm lying to you … after all of these years? I mean, come on, I died trying to bring your space shuttle back to you. Why would I lie now?"

I looked into Tom's serious eyes. Why would he steer me wrong? He never had before. But why was he so defensive?

My hand reached out and grabbed for the cigar. I stared at it. Reluctantly, I brought it to my mouth and took a puff. Just then, Tom reached out and patted me on the shoulder. With his touch, we were gone, leaving John behind.

CHAPTER SIXTEEN

Light after light illuminated the vast new area. There must have been a million peepholes floating along the wall that were now accessible. My eyes were drawn to all of them. It looked like outer space.

I took steps toward the lights, dragging my hand along the wall as I picked up my pace. Tom followed behind me. Finally, another adventure with my best friend. I knew what life was like without him and I wanted to enjoy every moment here with him, even though part of my mind had a really tough time accepting that this was Tom. I did my best to silence that part.

"Why are there so many?" I asked, amazed at how cool it looked. I spun in circles, trying to decide which one to look through.

"Tricks of being here for a while. I've got plenty more!" Tom said, still walking behind me. "Go ahead, check one out!"

I smiled and looked back at him. "What about this one?" I pointed to the peephole that was closest to me and inched my eye toward it.

"No!" Tom said, slightly raising his voice. "Not yet." He guided me farther along to a different one. "Look into this one."

Weird, what was in that one? I thought. I was slightly thrown off by Tom's reaction, but he must have known what he was doing. He had been here longer than me. I followed his order and approached the peephole that he wanted me to look through. Slowly, I put my eye to it.

"What do you see?" Tom asked with a little snicker in his voice, as if he knew that I would love what I was about to see.

"No way!" I yelled.

"I told you we'd go there together," Tom said, standing next to me.

I saw outer space. I looked out into a star-filled, night sky. There were planets in the distance and I had on a space suit. I could feel it!

"Open the door if you want," he said.

"What?" I pulled my eye away. "Door?" I was so confused. "But there aren't any knobs," I started to say, until I realized there was one on the door. I lit up with excitement. "How did you do that?"

"Go ahead," Tom reassured me, ignoring my question.

"Wait, where's John?" I asked in a moment of clarity.

Tom reached out, grabbed my hand, and opened the door. It was different than before. In addition to being able to see what was going on behind the peephole, I was able to physically be in that world. Tom and I were about to fulfill our promise of making it to space together. We were sitting in a space shuttle, ready for takeoff. I felt the weight of my massive space suit, the super tight seatbelt that had me strapped in, and the heat of the rocket on my butt that was about to send us into orbit. I reached up and touched my helmet, smudging my visor. Tom sat next to me. We were ready.

"3, 2, 1 ... " The countdown ticked down. "Blastoff!"

Fire lit below the shuttle. A rush of force sent us into the air. My face stretched from the smile that spread across my cheeks. It went from one of my ears to the other. Wow! I was so ready for space.

Tom looked over and watched my reaction. "We haven't even gotten there yet!"

The view, as we continued gaining altitude, was unbelievable. The pressure against my body was intense. The ship kept climbing and eventually, we escaped the atmosphere. We made it—we were in space!

"Open the door," Tom said.

"What? No. I can't do that. I'm not trying to get sucked into space."

"Haven't you always wanted to get out there … in space? To explore places that no one else ever has?" Tom asked as he sat strapped in next to me.

Should I? Tom reached over and unbuckled my seat belt, then he nodded. I mustered the courage, stood up, and approached the door. Slowly, I grabbed the lever to open the exit hatch and pulled it. I could feel the difference in pressure. I closed my eyes and took one step, then another, then another. When I finally opened my eyes, I was floating in space! *Ahhhhhh! This is so cool!* I cheered in my head.

The feeling was breathtaking. The world was quiet; I couldn't hear any sounds. Stars were all around me. It was peaceful—I was at peace. I lifted my visor and opened my mouth, trying to let all of the space air in.

It was the most incredible feeling and like nothing that I could have ever imagined. I leaned my head back, still smiling from ear to ear. I spread my arms and legs and flailed through space, like I was a kid with his best friend again and with no worries in the world. That feeling was short lived as something pulled me back by my neck.

I let out a slight cough and turned to see if Tom had grabbed me, but it wasn't him. It was my cape. I had been so happy with Tom that the power of the cape and helping John had completely slipped my mind.

Instantly, my space suit disappeared. The cord closed tighter around my neck. I reached up and grabbed at it, trying to free some extra space, but it wouldn't loosen. I tried stretching my neck, anything, to give myself more breathing room, but it didn't work.

My eyes searched for Tom. Where did he go? Was I out of time?

There he was. I reached out, pleading for help. Tom stared at me, watching me struggle. After what felt like forever, he finally reached out and took hold of me. Within seconds, we were back outside of the peephole that had led us into space. The area around us was still lit by the peepholes lining the wall. But the light from the one we had come out of went black. Again, I reached for the cord, realizing that it hadn't fully tightened yet. But it continued to close around my neck, serving as an unfriendly reminder that I was here for a different reason than to see space.

"That's temporary," Tom said, as he reached for the cord-like choker necklace that was around his own neck. "See this? It was my cord. I cut it off and wear it as a trophy now. It only takes a moment. You can decide on your own to stay here with me. Forget John, you can live freely in the In-Between. But if you wait until time expires, you'll be trapped, and we won't see each other ever again."

CHAPTER SEVENTEEN

The cord around my neck tightened a little bit more. It was enough to make me gag. Waves of warm panic rushed through my body. I was running out of air, lying on the floor of the dark tunnel. Tom paced back and forth in front of me, waiting for my decision. "Cut the cord, Matty. It'll be the best thing you ever did," he said, emphatically.

I was running out of time. The cord continued to get tighter and tighter. "Wait, where's John?" I choked out, while my eyes searched the area.

Tom kept pacing, pretending that he hadn't heard me. "Tom," I barely got out his name with a loud choke. "Where's John?" I used everything I had left to yell it out.

Tom definitely heard me this time. "I dunno, gone I guess."

He charged toward me, trying to reach out for the cord around my neck. I squirmed and dodged his initial attempts. "What's wrong with you?" I asked. Tom kept trying to grab hold of the cord.

Something wasn't right.

"Nothing. I just want you to stay here with me. I miss you and hate living life without you," Tom said, starting to get choked up. "All you have to do is cut the cord, and we'll be together forever. We can do anything. Look ..." he pointed to another peephole nearby. "You can still experience home here."

The cord had slowed its tightening for the moment. Perhaps it was giving me time to make a decision on whether or not to cut it off. My legs were weak and wobbly as I got to my feet. Slowly, I walked to the peephole that Tom was pointing to and looked through it.

I could see a bright, sunny day in a town that was very familiar to me. I saw a street that I knew very well. It was where I lived. Then I saw my bicycle, the one I loved to ride. I kept seeing more and more things that were familiar to me: my house, my parents' car, the garage, inside the house—the kitchen, the stairs, my bedroom door. It really felt like I was back home. I could even feel the blue carpet brush through my toes.

The door to my room was closed. I reached out and opened it. I looked at my shelves. My eyes looked at the top one—there was a space shuttle, but not just any shuttle; the one that Tom tried to bring back to me when he got hit by the truck. I pulled my head away.

"You can have it all here and you don't have to deal with the pain of the real world." Tom said. He must have known that my mind was in turmoil. "Imagine having your best friend back like nothing ever happened."

I was so conflicted. It would have been amazing to have Tom back, but something wasn't adding up.

"Look through the peephole again," he encouraged me.

I went back and put my eye to the peephole.

Tom was sitting on the bed. Again, I pulled away. All of this reminded me of how I felt before Tom had died.

"See, we can live life here as if we were back home," Tom said, really pushing for me to stay.

Of course, I wanted to have Tom back. It was so difficult living life without him, but I wanted Tom back in the real world. I didn't want to have to stay in the In-Between. I'd have to leave my family and they'd have to experience what

Tom's family had just gone through. I reminded myself of the promise I made to Joel. I couldn't stay here. I had to go back to the real world. Besides, nothing was exactly the same in the In-Between. It was close, but even Tom seemed a little different here.

Tom circled me, like a shark. "You can have your life back here, as if the accident never happened."

Ugh. It was all gut-wrenching. I was more confused here than in the real world.

"You're running out of time. Cut the cord." Tom was basically screaming at me as he reached into his sweatpants and pulled out a pocketknife. "You can do it." He put out his hand with the knife in it and passed it to me.

My arms were hidden behind the purple cape. Tom held the knife out, waiting for me to grab it. Slowly, I pulled my hand out from the cape and grabbed the knife. I looked at it resting in my right hand, ready to cut the cord. It felt basically weightless, even magical. I suspected that not just any knife would cut the cape's cord. This one seemed powerful.

I dropped my shoulders. I thought I wasn't going to do it, but with the knife in my hand, I was conflicted again. *Should I do it and accept my fate?* I thought. I reached my left hand up to the cord as it tightened again—even it was growing impatient—time to decide.

My hand freed just enough space to get the knife underneath the cord. I popped out the blade and brought it toward my neck. I slid the knife under the cord. The cold metal pressed tightly against my neck and the blade was ready to cut.

"Matty, wait!" A different, but very familiar voice called out to me in my head. It startled me and my hand slipped. A few threads of the cord came loose.

CHAPTER EIGHTEEN

There was a tear in the cord—threads hung loose, but it wasn't cut all the way through. I stopped myself from cutting more and turned toward the voice that I heard in my head.

I was overwhelmed. I couldn't believe what I was seeing.

Was it real?

"Tom?" I called out with confusion.

In front of me, to the left, was a mirror image of the Tom who had been guiding me through the In-Between. He even had on the same outfit: his blue Space Camp shirt and red sweatpants.

I looked left, then right. They were the same person. Both of them were my best friend. Which one was the real Tom?

It didn't take long for me to get my answer.

The first Tom's face grew angrier, then something started to change. He literally transformed into something else. Chills raced up my spine. I had been fooled! The first Tom grew to ten feet tall and became massive in stature. His red hair flowed past his shoulders and he wore a thick beard dark as night. A black cape covered his entire body. He smoked a cigar that looked like a tree trunk.

What was happening?

Even though I was still slightly skeptical, I sprinted toward the new Tom. Together, we ran as fast as we could away from the fake Tom.

Sensations of fear charged through my body. What was the spirit going to do to us? I looked at Tom, who was looking back at me. In my head, I could hear him talking to me. "Matty, I missed you."

"I know … I missed you too. This wasn't how it was supposed to be." It was Tom, the real Tom. I knew it. Seeing him made me remember all of the good times: our play dates, birthday parties, days at school, and Space Camp. I wanted all of that back so bad. Those were all of the feelings that I lacked with the fake Tom. I felt complete again with the real Tom. Being with him was 100% worth staying in the In-Between for.

I stopped running and reached the knife to the cord. *Yes, I am going to do this.* I thought.

"No! You can't," the real Tom screamed. "This isn't the real world. It'll never be the same."

I stopped myself from cutting the cord. "But life is terrible without you. I can't do it anymore."

"You have to live life for the both of us now. A *real* life. Accomplish all of our dreams." Tom hugged me. "You have to. It's not your time yet," he said, urging me to leave the In-Between.

"But what about you?" I asked.

"I'll always be with you for the rest of your life."

I clenched my jaw and wiped my eyes.

"I have a solution." The spirit said in a deep, raspy voice, interrupting our reunion. "Come with me," the spirit continued, using his hands to lure us over. "You both can live like kings in the Netherworld with me."

I looked at the spirit, then at Tom. Of course, I wanted to stay, but I couldn't go to the Netherworld. The previous Peephole Master warned me of that. Deep down, I knew Tom was right. I needed to get back to the real world. But how?

And John? Where was John?

"I was being nice in letting you feel like you had a choice. You're both coming with me regardless," the spirit called out as he threw the lit cigar toward us. The cigar flew by, barely missing direct contact with us. This spirit went into attack mode, storming toward us.

"Who are you?" I called out to the spirit.

"I'm Lord of the Netherworld and I'm here for your souls." The spirit came at us without moving his legs. He floated at an incredibly fast speed.

Without thinking, I reached out and grabbed Tom's shoulder. Tom and I were transported to another tunnel-like area. This one had a few peepholes lit up, but there was something else that I could sense. I could hear someone trying to communicate with me, and it wasn't Tom.

It was John!

Together, Tom and I navigated the darkness until we reached him. "What are you doing here?" I asked John, assuming that this new area was somehow related to Tom.

John shrugged his shoulders, looking lost.

I looked around and saw a peephole light up nearby. Perhaps that would give me some answers. As I took a few steps toward it, my throat tightened up again. The cord was closing in on me again. Each time that it did that, I worried that the cape would strangle me. I

91

fought through it and got on my tippy toes to see into the peephole. Something came over me, an aura of sorts. This seemed to be the peephole that I was brought here to see—the one that would have all of the answers. I put my eye to it.

It was nighttime in my neighborhood. Everything looked quiet—not many people were out on the roads, not much of anything was happening. Suddenly, there was a sense of disturbance and chaos in the air. I wandered through our small town with a bird's eye view of the area. I smelled smoke, but initially, I couldn't figure out exactly where it was coming from. I scanned the area until I located a fire. I got closer to it. It was the scene that I had already seen—the fire that Kevin had been a part of—the one that John never made it out of.

Why was I seeing this again? I already knew what happened.

Screeeeeeeeeeeeeeccccccccccccccccchhhhhhhhhhhh!

Tires squealed. The sound echoed through my ears, causing a fierce pain that nearly ripped me away from the peephole. But I was stuck here, glued in place—like how I felt at the cabin, when I was brought to the In-Between.

There was a bike on the ground—a bike that I recognized.

A space shuttle—not the real thing, but a diecast replica.

A boy lay in the street, screaming, crying.

Then I saw the vehicle—a red pickup truck.

CHAPTER NINETEEN

My stomach sank. This was the red pickup truck that had hit Tom—the vehicle responsible for killing my best friend. I followed it. I needed to know who was driving. I had to hold that person accountable for what had happened to Tom.

The red truck sped through stop signs, traffic lights, and took the turns really hard and fast. The driver was trying to escape the scene of the crime really fast. The truck kept getting closer and closer to the fire. Sirens from the fire trucks and emergency vehicles roared into my head as they rushed to the burning house.

The red pickup truck also abruptly stopped at the house.

The door ripped open. A man in a black hooded sweatshirt and dark blue jeans jumped out. I kept trying to get closer. Who was this? Finally, I saw his face. It was John.

"Nooooooooooooo!" I screamed, as I ripped my head away from the peephole. My voice echoed time and time again through the tunnel structure where we were stranded.

Angrily, I turned to John and grabbed him by the collar of his sweatshirt. I had no idea how strong I was in the In-Between. I lifted John off the ground with ease. He looked at me in horror. Tom panicked and tried to stop me. "Matty, what are you doing? What's wrong?"

"It was him. He drove the red truck. He killed you," I said in a fierce and evil voice. I could feel my body tightening with rage.

It was as if John had an epiphany. He didn't remember what happened until I reminded him.

Tom approached me from behind and eased my arms down, which lowered John back to the ground. John pleaded with me, "I'm so sorry. I promise. I didn't mean to hurt anybody. I was going to go back for him, I swear."

Furiously, I turned away from him.

Tom put his arm around me. "Hating him won't bring me back. It was my time and it was his time. We are forever connected."

"No." I said, sternly. "It's not fair." I had a hard time believing that Tom was okay with this. How was he so at peace with this situation? How was I supposed to look at, let alone help, the person who was responsible for killing my best friend?

John was still overcome. "No! Matty, I'm sorry," he pleaded. "I swear to you, I was going to go back. But I had to save my brother. He would've died. What would you have done if Tom had been in that fire? Would you have stopped?"

I put my head down. I didn't know how to answer that. I collapsed to my knees and tried to cry. I wanted to let all of this emotion out. But my head yanked back as the cord tightened its hold. I gasped for air.

Tom rushed over to me, pleading with me. "You have to help him. Only you know what he needs. Think Matty: you have to let this go. You can't bring me back."

My eyes dried as it felt like my life was being sucked out of me and that every breath would be my last. I motioned for John to come to me as I collapsed to the ground. I was running out of oxygen and time to think. It was now or never— I had to save John or stay in the In-Between forever.

John rushed over. "Matty, Tom, I know that you don't believe me, but I'm sorry, and I wish the accident never happened."

Tom broke down. Slowly, he reached out and shook John's hand. Tom nodded. "Thanks."

I struggled to lift my head, but I acknowledged the sincerity of John's apology. It was one of the hardest things I've ever done, but I got out the words: "Thank you. I forgive you."

Blinding, bright lights illuminated the dark area. A large *boom* went off like a bomb exploding, sending Tom and me flying backwards. The area spun faster and faster. The bright lights had a dizzying effect.

Was this it? Was I dead too?

I wanted to talk to Tom longer, but I couldn't. My eyes shut and my body was pulled in every direction.

CHAPTER TWENTY

Slowly, I came back to life. Cold, wet grass brushed against my face. My eyes begrudgingly opened. I lay face down in the woods. I picked up my head and looked around. I was back in the woods near the cabin.

Was I back for good? Was I no longer the Peephole Master? Was Tom gone?

Another yank pulled at my neck. The cape still choked me. I forced myself up off the ground. "Tom!" I yelled.

Nothing.

"No! I never got to say goodbye," I stammered. I had really wanted to say goodbye to my best friend. But again, that opportunity had been taken away from me.

Something grabbed me from behind. I shot around. It was Tom!

My body tingled with excitement as I could feel the widest grin spread across my face. I saw the same grin mirrored on Tom's face.

"You did it! I'm so proud of you … but now you have to go," Tom said.

Tears collected in my eyes. No. I didn't want our time together to end again. I realized that it was probably going to be the last time I ever saw Tom, but unlike the families whose loved ones pass suddenly, I was getting a chance to say goodbye one last time. "I love you like my brother," I said, struggling to get out the word *brother*, but I kept trying until I finally did. The stranglehold of the cord was the tightest it had been and it didn't help that tears poured down my face.

"You are my brother," Tom said.

I did my best to walk through the woods as slow as possible, knowing what was about to happen. Tom followed as we neared the cabin. He stopped and stared at it. "I'll never forget this place."

I sniffled and squinted my teary eyes. "Me neither." I reached out and started our shake: a light kick to the shin, an elbow tap, two fist pumps on our own fist, then a pat on the back.

I could hear him fight off his own tears as I pulled him in tight for a hug after the tap. When we stepped back from each other, I tried to take in the moment. I stared at my best friend in the entire world, fully knowing that this was it. It would be the last time I'd ever see him. But, I was so glad that we'd been able to live out one last adventure together.

The cape tightened once more, squeezing my neck like a vice clamp—it wasn't waiting any longer. My vision blurred. I knew it was the beginning of the end. My powers were weakening. I looked at Tom one last time and turned toward the cabin. The last lighted peephole was waiting for me so I could return to the real world. But I stopped dead with one last burst of adrenaline to fight off the cape choking me.

"Wait!" I called out, using everything that I had left. "Every time I look at my space shuttle or think about space, I'll think of you. And I promise that I'll accomplish all of our goals and dreams. I'll do it for both of us."

"I know you will! And even if you can't see me, I'll be right there with you!" Tom said. "Oh, and by the way, lose the glasses, they make your face look weird!" Even as he tried to make a joke, Tom's face had sadness written all over it.

I let out a slight smile, took the glasses off my face, stuffed them into my pocket, and gave him one last look at my regular eyes.

I turned and stepped on the deck before putting my eye to the peephole.

CHAPTER TWENTY ONE

Bammmm! Bammm! Bammm! A pounding noise came from nearby.

Someone knocked on the door.

I rolled around, slowly waking up.

Where was I?

My eyes adjusted to the bright sun entering the room. I was in my sleeping bag at the log cabin. The knocking continued. What now? I sat up and stared at the door. I couldn't help but be freaked out. Who would be here? No one even knew about the cabin.

Was last night real? Tom, John, the Peephole Master, the Lord of the Netherworld? Was that all a dream or had I actually lived it?

Bammm! Bammm! More knocks. Whoever was at the door wasn't going away.

Joel rushed into the main area from the back deck, rubbing his tired eyes. "Who's knocking?

"I dunno. Look through the peephole." I said, pointing to the door.

"What peephole?" Joel asked, looking at the wooden door. There wasn't a peephole anywhere to be found.

"Huh," I said, sitting up in my sleeping bag. Finally, I shot up and beat Joel to the door, opening it quickly. No one was there. Joel poked his head out and didn't see anyone either. He went back inside, while I scoured the area.

A branch snapped nearby. There was a girl. She saw me and walked toward the cabin. Weirdly, she looked so familiar to me: strawberry blonde hair, toothpick arms and legs, and freckles all over her face.

"You knocked?" I asked her.

"Nice to see you on this side, Matty," the girl with the yellow eyes said.

No way! It was the former Peephole Master. What was she doing here?

I smiled and nervously dove my hands into my pockets. "Hi," I said as my hand felt something. A rush of adrenaline shot through my insides. My face must've shown a sense of panic.

"What's wrong?" she asked.

I pulled out what was in my pocket. The glasses.

The Peephole Master glasses.

"Oh no, I don't think you were supposed to keep those," she said with a look of fright.

Check out the winning story
from the

FRIGHTVISION

Writing Contest for Kids:

Just the Two of Us
written by:
Jasmine Robinson (age 12)
from Mount Dora, FL

JUST THE TWO OF US

Okay, before we start, let's get one thing straight: I'm not going to start this off like every other horror story out there. "It was a dark and stormy night, blah blah blah…" Well, if I'm being honest, it was a pretty clear night. I mean you could see the stars and the moon was shining bright.

I was riding my bike over to the store to get some chips (my parents were out and I was heading to my friend's house) when I saw this weird blue light coming from off in the distance. And suddenly, I blacked out. I mean like, just all of the sudden Bam! I was out.

I woke up … um… Somewhere?

It looked like some time had passed, because the stars had definitely shifted. I looked around, and I was in a forest. I guess I wasn't that far in, because I could still see the light from the gas station beaming through the trees.

I checked my pocket and my phone was still there, but the battery was dead. I didn't know what to do or what had just happened, but I wasn't really panicking. Of course, I was scared, but I was mostly just wondering how I got out here.

I stood up and started walking towards the light, and after a few minutes I broke out of the forest. I looked around and sure enough there was my bike. And just my luck, it was totally trashed. I mean the handlebar was bent and everything. Just great.

I picked it up and walked it over by the bike lock next to the building. I still had my money, so I went into the gas station store to grab some chips. I figured if I hurried, I could still make it to my friend's house and apologize for being late. Strange thing is, when I got inside, nobody was there. I figured they just weren't busy this late at night and that's why there weren't any cars. But this was open 24 hours, and the lights were still on so I thought someone would be there. I just left the money on the counter and took the snacks and left.

I bent the handlebar back into place and tried to ride back to my neighborhood, though the trip was painfully slow. I got to the sidewalk and rode past Melanie and Tori's house. It was weird because every Friday night they were always having some type of party. I mean their cars were home and everything. I finally got to Jaiden's house and I knocked on the door. No response. It's fine, she's probably just in the bathroom.

I waited a minute and knocked again. No response. I almost rang the doorbell, but I decided to try the door. It was unlocked. I went in, because I figured they had at least heard me by now.

I stepped inside, apologizing for barging in, but it appeared I was saying sorry to no one. Now this was especially weird because her dads were always watching the latest football games together. But, who knows, maybe they were in the kitchen, or talking to Jaiden, or worse; calling my mom. I brushed that thought out of my mind as I walked down the hall into the kitchen. No one. 'Okay', I thought, 'just keep looking around, maybe they're outside'? I stepped onto the back porch, and to no surprise, nobody was there. I ran back and forth checking every room there was, but to no avail.

Now I was really panicking. I locked the front door and rode my bike to the one place I knew there had to be people. The mall. It took me almost half an hour to get over there (thank God for the bike lane) and by the time I got to the parking lot, I was out of breath and panting like a dog.

I took a minute to catch my breath, and went in. I took one look at the place and just like everywhere else, it was empty. I mean this is the MALL we're talking about. When have you ever seen one empty? Especially on a Friday night?! Where was everyone?

Wait! I still have my phone on me! I rushed to the food court to find one of those little stations where you can plug your phone in. I plugged it in and couldn't wait till it hit enough charge to text someone. I pulled up the Messages app and texted my mom. No response. I tried Jaiden. Nothing. I gave up. I didn't know what to do. It's like everyone had disappeared.

I slumped against the wall, and I looked over the food court. That's when I saw her.

Long, dark hair, a tattered black dress, and glowing, blue eyes that shone through all the hair in her face. She was tall, and skinny, with spindly fingers that ended with sharp claws.

I ducked behind the table next to me, hoping she didn't see me. I was wrong. She was quicker than lighting and was behind the table in a flash. This was that weird light I saw earlier.

I tried to keep my breathing quiet, in hopes that maybe she would walk away, maybe, just maybe, she wouldn't be interested in killing me.

But just then, I got an alert from my phone. Great. She whipped her head around, staring at me with those bright blue eyes...and that was it.